Let's Go, Philadelphia!

YEARLING BOOKS are designed especially to entertain and enlighten young people. Patricia Reilly Giff, consultant to this series, received her bachelor's degree from Marymount College and a master's degree in history from St. John's University. She holds a Professional Diploma in reading and a Doctorate of Humane Letters from Hofstra University. She was a teacher and reading consultant for many years, and is the author of numerous books for young readers.

A Polk Street Special

Let's Go, Philadelphia!

Patricia Reilly Giff

Illustrated by Blanche Sims

A Yearling Book

Published by
Bantam Doubleday Dell Books for Young Readers
a division of
Bantam Doubleday Dell Publishing Group, Inc.
1540 Broadway
New York, New York 10036

ISBN: 0-440-41368-0
Printed in the United States of America
May 1998
10 9 8 7 6 5 4 3
CWO

To Wendy Lamb
with admiration

From Mrs. Miller's Book:

OLDEN DAYS IN OLD
PHILADELPHIA

When our country was new, Philadelphia was the place to be. It was an exciting city. Many people said it was the most important city. It was the place where the United States began.

William Penn had gotten the land from the king of England. He called it *the City of Brotherly Love.*

It was the place where Thomas Jefferson

wrote the Declaration of Independence. The Declaration said that all men were free.

It was the place where our first laws were written.

It was the place where Benjamin Franklin lived. And everyone knows he was always trying new things.

Chapter 1

It was Something New Week at the Polk Street School.

Richard "Beast" Best dashed down the street. He could see Mrs. Miller's black car parked near the school gate.

"Uh-oh," he told Matthew. Mrs. Miller, the Killer, was the worst substitute teacher in the school.

They turned into the schoolyard.

Beast was wearing a yucko birthday scarf today. But it was something new.

"Hey, Beast." Matthew grabbed the yucko scarf.

"Yeow," Beast yelled.

The scarf came loose. It dropped in a puddle.

Beast banged open the door. He kept laughing while Matthew fished out the scarf.

They flew up the stairs with it . . . and into Room 113.

"This is not a circus," said someone in a loud voice. "But I see a couple of clowns."

Beast stopped on one foot.

It was Mrs. Miller, the Killer.

"Where's Ms. Rooney?" Beast asked.

"Home with a cold today," said Mrs. Miller.

Good thing it was only one day, Beast thought.

The class was getting ready for a trip . . . a trip to Philadelphia.

Beast dragged the scarf down the aisle. It dripped all the way.

"Are you two last every day?" Mrs. Miller asked.

"Yes," said Dawn Bosco. She was wearing new barrettes. They looked like pink ears.

Mrs. Miller made caterpillar eyebrows at them. "I'm astounded," she said.

Beast slid into his seat. He drew a picture of himself in a skinny scarf.

He started to laugh.

Mrs. Miller was watching.

He snapped his mouth shut. He looked up at the red sign on the board:

TRY SOMETHING NEW WEEK
IN MS. ROONEY'S ROOM.

It was because of Philadelphia. "When our country was young," Ms. Rooney had said, "people in Philadelphia were always trying something new."

He and Matthew were doing something else new. It was at home instead of school.

It was a surprise for Beast's father.

They were fixing up the garage.

Right now the garage was a mess. There wasn't even room for the car.

He and Matthew had started to paint yesterday.

The painting part was more fun than the cleaning.

They were going to clean last.

The best part was that the paint was orange. Matthew had a ton of it left over from something.

Orange was a great color.

A spectacular color.

Beast looked down at his feet. His sneakers had orange drips all over them.

One drip sneaker had been a mistake. The other he had done on purpose.

Now they matched . . . new orange drip sneakers.

Beast closed his eyes.

He could see the garage in his head. The walls. The floor.

Everything orange except the ceiling.

They'd never get up that high.

He could see his father opening the doors someday.

He'd be astounded.

Beast looked down at his hands. A couple of spots of orange paint. But mostly mud.

Maybe he should go down the hall. Wash them off.

Too late. Mrs. Miller was standing up. "You are so lucky," she said. "I've always wanted to go to Philadelphia."

Emily raised her hand. She was wearing a new spider ring. "They were always doing something new in Philadelphia," she said.

In back of him, Dawn was breathing like a horse. "We know that already," she whispered. She waved her hand. "It's a city in Pennsylvania."

"Named after William Penn," said Mrs. Miller.

Beast gave Matthew a poke. "Sounds as if it was named after a pencil."

Mrs. Miller was smiling. She looked like a shark with all those teeth.

Beast rubbed his hands together. The mud was dry now. It came off in dots on his desk.

Mrs. Miller began to talk about someone named Benjamin Franklin. "He was always making something new," she said. "Inventing things."

She leaned forward. "He was really poor.

There were seventeen children in his family. But never mind. He worked hard. He flew a kite in a thunderstorm."

Beast made a mud dot face on the desk.

"Benjamin put a key on the end of a kite string," Mrs. Miller said.

She clapped her hands hard.

Everyone jumped.

"*Boom*," yelled Mrs. Miller. "A flash of lightning. A spark from the key . . ." She stopped. "What did that mean?"

"It meant lightning was electricity," said Timothy Barbiero, the smartest kid in the class.

"Now you're talking," said Mrs. Miller.

Beast thought about fooling around with electricity in a thunderstorm. His mother would have a fit.

He guessed Mrs. Miller was talking about that new kid, Benjamin, in his sister Holly's class. He had come from Philadelphia. Holly said he was always making stuff.

"Maybe you could write a report," Mrs. Miller was saying. "Tell about someone in Philadelphia."

Beast started to breathe like a horse. So did Matthew. Mrs. Miller was still talking. Beast made a mud dot horse on his desk.

"I could give a prize," Mrs. Miller said.

Beast looked up.

"It would be as easy as riding a bike," she said.

A bike? he thought.

Everyone else was looking up too. Timothy. Noah. All the smart kids.

Beast started to breathe like a horse again. He'd never win a prize.

Chapter 2

Beast stood at the garage door. He looked back.

Holly wasn't near the kitchen window.

Good. Otherwise she'd be outside checking up on him. She thought she was his mother.

"Come on, Matthew," he whispered.

They were inside the garage in two seconds.

Beast looked down at the can. "We have

to swirl the paint around." He reached for a stick.

"I think some bugs have drowned in it," Matthew said.

Beast waved his hand. "Don't worry. They'll just look like orange dots."

He pointed with the stick. "I'm going to start over there."

Too bad Holly's wreck of a blue bike was in the way. He gave it a little shove.

It slammed down on the paint can.

"Don't worry," he told Matthew again. "She won't even notice a drop or two."

He spun the tire with one finger and looked around for a brush.

"Stiff as a board." Matthew held the brush up. "I think we should have washed it out."

Beast grunted. He found a second brush. That was stiff as a board too. He put the bike back on its kickstand. It wobbled.

He reached in between Holly's bike. He dipped the brush into the open paint can. "Nice and wet." He began to hum. "Looks like new."

Mrs. Miller was right. New things were astounding.

Matthew was humming too. "Just a couple of days to Philadelphia," he said. "I'm dying to see it."

Beast thought back to what Ms. Rooney had told them. "A man named William Penn started Philadelphia. He wanted it to be a place of no fighting."

Beast brushed paint on the wall.

Ms. Rooney had told them there was a building with a statue of William Penn on top. "William's hat was the highest spot in the city for a long time," she had said. "No one would build anything higher."

Beast couldn't wait to see it.

"What did Benjamin invent, anyway?" he

asked Matthew. "Besides that electricity stuff?"

Matthew stopped painting. He wiped at a line of paint on the wall. "This is going to look great," he said.

"What did Benjamin invent?" Beast began again.

Matthew raised one shoulder. "Never even heard of—" He stepped back, back against Holly's bike, back against the paint can.

"Watch out," Beast shouted.

It was too late. The bike fell. The paint can tipped.

"Yeow," Matthew yelled. Thick orange paint covered the floor.

It covered Holly's fender too.

Beast could hardly swallow. He reached out. He touched one wheel. "Sopping wet."

Poor old Holly Polly, he thought. The

bike was the worst wreck he had ever seen. Much worse than before.

He thought about Benjamin again. Benjamin would try something new. Maybe he'd paint . . .

"I'm thinking of something," he said to Matthew. "Something astounding."

"Me too," said Matthew. "We could paint—"

"Part of it," Beast cut in. "Leave part blue. Kind of stripes . . . with orange drip wheels."

Holly would be thrilled. He could see her riding along on her new orange bike. Her crinkly hair would be streaming out in back of her.

Yes. Astounding.

"Here we go," said Beast. "Dr. Paint-Her-Up-Like-New." He tried to wiggle his eyebrows like Mrs. Miller.

They started to paint. One fender. The wheels. The handlebars.

"Lots of orange," Beast said. "New like Philadelphia was."

"New and exciting," said Matthew.

It was true. This was the most exciting thing he had ever done.

He made a paint dot face on the old blue seat.

He stepped back.

Matthew stepped back too.

They looked at each other.

"Great," Matthew said.

"Horrible," Beast said.

"It's different." Matthew touched the handlebars. "All dots and streaks."

"Are you kidding?" Beast said. "It's terrible."

Matthew sighed. "I think I have to go home now. Start getting ready for the trip to Philadelphia."

Beast rubbed his hands against his jeans.

He rolled Holly's bike into the back of the garage.

Orange bike tracks were all over the place.

He wondered what Holly was going to say when she found out.

He felt a lump in his throat.

He went into the house. He had to get ready too.

Chapter 3

B east was on his way to school.
He was carrying his books in an almost empty Frosted Flakes box.

It was something new. His books just fit . . . and he could eat the rest of the Frosted Flakes when he got hungry.

He was walking two steps in back of Holly.

She had to help him cross at Linden

Street. His mother thought he was still a big baby.

He took a quick look. Holly was slurping down an orange ice Blast-Off Bar.

"You're not supposed to eat ice on the way to school," he told her. He said it nicely, though.

He was never going to fight with Holly again. That would be something new.

Holly bit off an orange chunk. "Who says?"

She said it nicely too.

She didn't know she had the worst bike in the whole world.

Holly's best friend, Joanne, was waiting at the corner. "Hey," she yelled. "Tomorrow we go to Philadelphia."

Beast blinked. He had forgotten the fourth grade was going too.

That meant Holly.

Never mind that now. He had to win Mrs. Miller's prize for Holly.

And never mind that he wasn't the smartest kid in the class . . . probably not even medium smart. Somehow he and Matthew had to get that bike.

He caught up with her and Joanne.

"What about Benjamin?" he called.

"What about him?" Holly said over her shoulder.

"Does he have a bunch of kids in his family?"

Joanne was talking. "I can't wait to see the Delaware River, and the houses all stuck together in rows. . . ."

"About seventeen kids?" Beast asked.

"I can't wait either," Holly said. "That place had the first zoo. The first library . . ."

"It was the first capital of the country,"

said Joanne. She looked as if she knew everything in the world.

He spoke up louder. "How about telling me something he made?"

Holly sighed. "We're trying to tell you about Philadelphia," she said. "If you'd listen."

Joanne shook her head. "What a pest. And look at his sneakers. Orange dots all over them, like chicken pox."

"It's *something new*," he said. "An orange dot invention."

"Well . . . ," Holly said, "the sneakers are kind of interesting. Different."

He gave Holly a tap. "Tell me one thing Benjamin made," he said. "You know. Something like electricity."

"What are you talking about?" Holly looked up at the sky. "He made a tower out of toilet paper rolls. It was a huge thing."

"Benjamin told me about that too," said

Joanne. "He made it when he lived in Philadelphia."

Now Beast could hear the bell. Everyone
started to run.

He ran too. A tower of toilet paper rolls.
He couldn't believe it.

It was probably as big as the Polk Street
School.

He slid into the classroom.

Ms. Rooney was sitting at her desk. Her
nose was pink. Her eyes were red.

But she was back.

Astounding.

He sank down in his seat. He thought
about the bike prize.

He closed his eyes.

He could see Mrs. Miller wheeling it out.
It was black. It had a yellow seat.

Maybe she'd have a helmet to match the
seat.

Holly would hate black and yellow.

Too bad. She'd have to share. That was what she was always telling him.

He bit his knuckle. When would Mrs. Miller give them the bike?

They'd be in Philadelphia.

Then the weekend would come.

Maybe she'd forget about the whole thing.

Just then the classroom door opened. It was Mrs. Miller.

Beast sat up straight. He tried to think about how to ask about the bike.

"I came with a book," Mrs. Miller told Ms. Rooney. *"Olden Days in Old Philadelphia.* A great book."

"Lovely," said Ms. Rooney.

Mrs. Miller began to read. It was about the king of England. He gave William Penn a pile of land to make Philadelphia.

Beast leaned forward. He shot a lunch bag rubber band at Matthew.

Matthew looked back. *"Shoom,"* he said.

Mrs. Miller stopped reading. She was making caterpillar eyebrows again. "Philadelphia was special because—" she began.

"It was a whole new thing," said Beast quickly. "People tried to like each other. They tried not to fight."

"They tried to share new ideas," Timothy broke in.

Mrs. Miller nodded. "Right."

Ms. Rooney's eyes were closing.

"And," said Beast, "there's going to be a prize."

"Right," said Mrs. Miller again.

Beast opened his mouth. He was about to ask when they'd get the prize. But he had a better idea.

"Why don't you come with us?" he said. "Bring the prize along."

Ms. Rooney's eyes flew open.

Matthew slid down in his seat.

Mrs. Miller blinked. "I'm astounded," she said. "I'll do it. I'll even sit with you on the bus."

Beast sat back. He couldn't believe it. He'd have to sit with Mrs. Miller.

It was worth it, he thought. As long as he got the bike for Holly.

Chapter 4

It was Friday. Trip day.

Everyone was racing around the schoolyard. They were waiting for the bus to come.

Beast was racing too. But he was racing carefully. He had his "New Things About Philadelphia" report under his arm.

Mrs. Miller had told them they'd read the reports on the bus.

Beast took a breath. His report was terrific. He had written all about Benjamin and the huge toilet paper roll tower.

He had put in some extra things too. A clothespin. He had seen a giant one in a book about Philadelphia. The clothespin was standing up in front of a building.

Who knew why?

He had put in stuff about pretzels too. Holly had told him people in Philadelphia loved fat pretzels. They ate them with mustard.

Matthew had drawn the cover. It was yellow with purple lines like lightning.

Emily Arrow ran by. She was wearing a clunky bracelet. It looked as if it belonged to her mother. It was probably something new.

Matthew was shouting in his ear. "Philadelphia, here we come." He was wearing his father's tie.

"A couple of gravy stains," Matthew said. "But it's new for me."

Beast nodded. He saw Mrs. Miller across the yard. He stopped. He had forgotten they'd have to sit with her.

"At least we'll win the bike," he said.

Suppose they didn't?

"Maybe we'll win," Matthew said. "And maybe not."

"For Holly," Beast said.

"What do you mean?" Matthew said. "For the three of us. To share."

Beast looked over toward the fence. He could see Holly reading.

Holly had her nose in a book every minute. She was always telling him about what she read.

Now Emily Arrow was back. "I'm going to tell about Thomas Jefferson," she said. "He was a great guy."

"Not as great as Benjamin," Beast said.

"No," said Matthew.

"Thomas helped get us free from the English," Emily told them. She clinked her bracelet. "He wrote this thing called the Declaration of Independence."

Beast shook his head. "Too bad he didn't call it something easy, like 'Freedom Report.'"

"Or 'Get Out of Here, English,'" said Matthew. He gave Beast a little punch and raced away.

Beast chased after him.

The bus pulled up. His report flew out of his hand.

Good thing he and Matthew were fast. Fast as the wind.

They scooped the pages up.

Holly's class climbed on first. They were sitting in the back.

Beast went to the end of the line. He tried to see if there was a bike inside the bus.

"It's probably underneath," Matthew said. "There's a space for suitcases and things."

Beast crossed his fingers.

He could see Matthew's fingers were crossed too.

They climbed up the bus steps.

Chapter 5

It was a great bus, Beast thought, with dark red seats.

Matthew whispered over his shoulder, "I'm sitting next to the window. You're in the middle. Mrs. Miller sits on the end."

Beast looked over his shoulder too.

Mrs. Miller was getting on the bus. She had a huge bag in her hand. "Prunes, apricots, and figs," she said. "A special treat."

The seats didn't look as great anymore. How would the three of them all fit? Beast wondered.

He found out a moment later. He was squished between Matthew and Mrs. Miller.

Dawn was sitting in back of them. "I guess I'm going to win the prize," she said. "I know all about the Liberty Bell when it was new . . . when it was old. The whole thing."

Beast twisted his neck. He didn't twist it far. There was hardly enough room to move.

He could see Dawn was wearing Liberty Bell earrings.

He could hear her too. She was the first to give her report.

"The Liberty Bell was made when the United States was becoming a country," Dawn said in a loud voice. "It was made even before that guy wrote the Declaration of Independence."

"Thomas Jefferson?" said Timothy.

Beast looked out the window. They turned onto the highway. The bus bumped along. It made a ton of noise.

"The bell is cracked." Dawn was almost yelling. "It doesn't ring anymore. It stands for freedom."

She cleared her throat. "The end."

Beast closed his eyes. Maybe he should have put in something about the Liberty Bell.

His father had told him all about it last night.

"The Americans were trying to get free from England," he had said. "They were going to have a war. They hid the bell on a farm. They were afraid the English would melt it down. They might even make bullets out of it."

Yes, Beast thought. When it was his turn he'd better add in that bell. Everyone thought it was important.

"Who wants to read next?" Ms. Rooney called.

Beast ducked his head. He wasn't so hot at reading aloud.

He took an apricot from Mrs. Miller's bag. It was a something-new snack.

Emily Arrow's hand shot up. She told about the Declaration of Independence.

"Thomas Jefferson didn't type it," she said. "He wrote it with a pen in just two weeks. A bunch of guys signed it. They sent it to the king of England."

Beast could hardly hear her. The bus motor was loud. Really loud.

So was Holly's class in back.

He took a prune next. He thought about giving his report.

It had to be perfect.

Noah and Timothy read their reports.

He couldn't hear a word.

Neither could anyone else.

Good. They'd never get the prize.

Even Ms. Rooney was shaking her head.

And next to him Mrs. Miller was sound asleep. He could hear her snoring.

She was even leaning her head toward him.

He was almost sitting on top of Matthew.

Then it was his turn.

Beast looked down at the floor in front of him. He couldn't even reach the report.

One of his arms was trapped in back of Mrs. Miller.

"I guess I'll tell the report," he said.

He told them about Benjamin . . . all the children in his family . . . and one of his inventions.

"A toilet paper roll tower," he said. "It's as big as . . ."

He tried to think.

"Bigger than . . ."

"The Empire State Building?" Matthew said.

"Well," Beast said, "it's as big as the Liberty Bell."

No one was listening.

"The end," said Beast. He felt wonderful. He had even gotten in the Liberty Bell.

He took a fig from Mrs. Miller's bag.

Up in front, Ms. Rooney was talking to the bus driver.

"Wait a minute," Dawn said. "Toilet paper rolls? I don't think they had toilet paper rolls in Benjamin Franklin's day."

"What is she saying?" Matthew asked. "It's so noisy."

"What do you mean?" Beast said. "He's not dead."

"Good grief," said Dawn Bosco. "Benjamin Franklin's been dead for about two hundred years."

Beast swiveled around as far as he could. He made sure he didn't wake Mrs. Miller.

Dawn had on her know-it-all face. "I don't think you're talking about the right one. You're talking about Benjamin Lee, in Holly's class."

Chapter 6

Just then Mrs. Miller woke up.

She raised her head. "Look, everyone," she said.

Beast stretched his neck to see what was going on.

He saw where Mrs. Miller was pointing.

"Philadelphia," he said.

"Well, you got that right, anyway," Dawn said.

He looked at the buildings in front of them.

They were tall with round or pointed tops. The colors were rose and green and gray.

The windows were like mirrors. He could see the sun and clouds floating in them.

The bus was slowing down. It turned up a wide street. "Next stop," said Ms. Rooney, "the Liberty Bell."

Beast and Matthew looked at each other.

They were both thinking about that Benjamin Lee business.

How could he have mixed all that up?

Would Mrs. Miller still give them the prize?

Beast pictured Holly's bike in the garage. An orange-striped mess.

They had to get the prize.

Who was Benjamin Franklin, anyway? he wondered.

Suddenly he thought of something. He took a breath.

Mrs. Miller had slept through their whole report.

Ms. Rooney had been talking to the bus driver.

No one else could even hear them over the noise of the bus.

No one but Dawn.

Would she tell?

He thought about it. Most of the time Dawn was a tattletale. Sometimes she wasn't.

He just had to keep his fingers crossed.

The bus stopped under a tree. The doors opened.

Ahead of them was a low building, long and plain. It was filled with people.

"Come on," he told Matthew.

They dashed ahead of Mrs. Miller. They shot through the door.

It would be terrible if everyone in Philadelphia thought Mrs. Miller was their partner.

"Wait up," Dawn was calling. "I want to talk to you."

They didn't wait. They circled around a group of people.

They landed in front of the bell.

It was big and brown. Beast could see the crack running down the side.

He could see that someone had tried to fix it.

Words were on the top. They were too hard to read.

The guard read aloud for them. " 'To proclaim liberty throughout the land . . .' Do you know what that means?" He smiled. "It means to tell everyone that America is a free land."

Beast nodded. "Like the Declaration of Independence."

"Close your eyes," the guard said. "Can't you picture the bell ringing?"

"*Bong*," said Beast.

"Never mind *bong*," said Dawn next to them. "I have to talk to you."

Beast swallowed. "Listen," he said. "I need that prize."

Dawn opened her mouth.

"Shhh," said Mrs. Miller. "Pay attention."

Then Ms. Rooney called the class. "We're going to walk to Independence Hall," she said. "It's the place where our country was born."

Timothy Barbiero nodded. "A lot of new things happened there. George Washington was made the head of the army to fight the English. . . ."

"The Declaration of Independence was signed there," Emily said.

Dawn touched her earrings. "Give me the Liberty Bell," she said.

"Give me Benjamin," Beast said.

"You mean Benjamin *Franklin*," Dawn said.

Beast touched the bell with one finger. He edged away from Dawn.

"Hey, wait up," she said.

He didn't stop. He sped out the door.

Chapter 7

They walked through a garden. Beast walked backward along the brick path.

He bumped into Matthew. "It's a new way of walking," he said. "But not so great."

They went inside Independence Hall.

"A group of men met here," another guard said. "They talked and argued about how to run our new country. Then they listened to each other. They made up rules.

They called them the Constitution. They were the first laws for America. We still use them."

Dawn Bosco raised her hand. "Benjamin Franklin was here too, right?"

"Right," said the guard.

Beast could see Dawn staring at him.

His mouth felt dry. Suppose she told everyone about his toilet paper roll report?

They'd think he was crazy.

Holly would say he should have thought about what he was doing.

He walked outside with Matthew and Mrs. Miller.

Then they were back on the bus again.

"You're going to love this next part," said Ms. Rooney. "We're going to see the Franklin Institute Science Museum."

"Named after Benjamin Franklin," Dawn said to Beast. "In case you didn't know."

"That Benjamin Franklin," Mrs. Miller said. "What a terrific inventor."

She held out the bag of fruit. "He made a stove to keep people warm. He made a tool to get books down from high shelves."

"I'm astounded," Matthew said.

"Now you're talking," said Beast.

Matthew grinned at him.

Beast tried to grin back. All he could think of was a silly toilet paper roll tower.

He wondered how he could have thought it was important.

Maybe Joanne was right.

Maybe he was a big pest.

He had never thought about being a pest before.

It was something new. And not so great either.

Inside the Franklin Institute, kids were running all over the place.

Some of them were looking at planes hanging from the ceiling.

In two seconds he and Matthew climbed a bunch of stairs.

They sat in the cockpit of a plane.

Everything looked different from up there. The floor below. The kids.

Something new popped into his head again.

"Pshoom." He aimed a make-believe gun at Dawn.

She didn't see him.

"She doesn't know she was just wiped out," Matthew said.

"You think she'll tell Mrs. Miller about our report?" Beast asked.

Matthew raised a shoulder in the air. "If she does, goodbye bike."

They walked down the stairs again.

"I have a great idea," Beast said. "We'll tell Dawn we'll share the bike with her too."

He looked up at Alex Walker.

Alex was shooting at him from the plane.

Lucky Alex. He didn't have to worry about a bike.

Beast made believe he was jumping away from a bullet. Matthew jumped away too.

"Listen, Matthew," he said. "Here's what we'll do. I'll have the bike on Monday. Tuesday it's for you. Wednesday and Thursday for Holly. Friday for Dawn."

Matthew was frowning. "I hate Tuesday."

Beast waved his hand. "You can have the weekend. Whatever you want."

He slid down in a seat near a window. In front of him were the controls of a plane.

"See if you can make this baby fly," said Matthew.

Beast pushed a button. It felt as if he were the pilot. He was looking out the plane window.

He could see the ground falling away.

He felt as if he were in the clouds.

"Watch out," said Matthew.

Beast saw a building coming up. He pushed another button fast.

He could hear a bell. "Crash," he said.

"Splat," said Matthew.

Beast stood up.

He wandered along the hall.

Mrs. Miller was sitting in front of a screen. "When I push this button . . . ," she began.

Crash, Beast said in his head.

"I'll see how I'll look when I get old," she said.

Beast bit his lip.

Mrs. Miller was old already.

She pushed the button.

She just looked older.

"Horrible," she said. But she was smiling a little. "A new look for me."

"You don't look so bad," he said.

He thought about it. She really didn't look that bad when she smiled.

Smiling might be a new thing for her.

He opened his mouth and shut it again.

"What?" she asked.

"You're pretty good when you smile."

"Really?" She smiled again.

Beast shook his head. Mrs. Miller wanted to look nice. What a surprise.

For a moment they didn't say anything. Then she waved her hand. "Isn't this a wonderful place?"

"Lots of new stuff," he said. "It makes me think about a bicycle."

"A bike? Really?" She made caterpillar eyebrows.

"My sister's bike is a wreck," he said. "A big wreck."

"Too bad," Mrs. Miller said.

"Yes," said Beast.

They stood there for another minute.

"Have you been in the heart yet?" Mrs. Miller asked.

"What heart?"

"It's in the next hall. It's huge. You can go inside." She smiled again. "You'll see what's going on in your own heart."

"I'll try it out."

He started for the heart. Dawn was in back of him. Her heels were clicking.

Beast made believe he didn't hear.

"Wait up," she yelled.

He quick-stepped down the hall. He raced up the stairs into a huge red heart.

He hid inside. The heart was all around him. It was red and pink with lines. He guessed the lines were supposed to be blood. Veins.

Dawn found him a minute later.

"About time I got to talk to you," she said.

"Don't worry," he said. "We're going to share the prize."

She waved her hand. "My report is better. Much better. It's not a thing about toilet paper rolls."

She shook her head. The Liberty Bell earrings dangled. "I get the prize, whatever it is."

"A bike," he said.

Dawn blinked. "A bike. I never won anything. And now I'm getting a bike?"

He swallowed. "Yes," he said.

Chapter 8

They were standing on the sidewalk. The street was filled with stores.

"See the archway?" Ms. Rooney pointed. "Over that alley?"

Beast looked up. A piece of wood was curved over a skinny path.

"Benjamin Franklin walked under there every day," Dawn said.

"His home was in back of the alley," said Ms. Rooney.

The class passed under the arch.

"No bike," Beast told Matthew. "No prize. No nothing."

"Why not?" Matthew said. "Just because—"

"Because of Dawn," Beast said.

"Holly's going to be mad," said Matthew.

"Holly's going to be sad," Beast said.

Just then Holly's class walked under the arch too.

Holly was reading something. She looked up. "Neat, right?" she said, and looked down at her book again.

Beast saw that her book was all about Benjamin Franklin.

A boy was marching along in back of Holly.

He was a long, skinny kid. He was wearing a button that said BEN.

Matthew rolled his eyes. "Benjamin Lee, I guess."

They followed the class down the alley into the back.

"The house is gone now," Ms. Rooney said. "But Benjamin Franklin lived right here."

"Can you just imagine?" Mrs. Miller said.

Beast looked around. "Astounding."

The class went down a stairway.

"There's an underground museum here," said Mrs. Miller. "It's about Benjamin's life."

A picture of Benjamin was hanging on the wall.

Beast stopped to look at him.

Benjamin was bald on top. He had long gray hair hanging down on the sides.

He looked like a nice old grandfather.

Almost like Mrs. Miller.

A moment later Dawn and Matthew were standing next to him. Mrs. Miller was telling them a story.

"You know, Benjamin was a little silly sometimes," she said.

"Like Beast," Dawn said.

"I am not . . . ," Beast began, then closed his mouth.

He thought about the toilet paper roll tower.

He looked down at his orange dot sneakers.

"Well, maybe," he said.

"Yup." Matthew made caterpillar eyebrows like Mrs. Miller. "Dr. Paint-Her-Up-Like-New," he whispered under his breath.

"Benjamin's brother James had a newspaper," said Mrs. Miller. "Benjamin made up funny letters. He signed them 'Mrs. Silence Dogood.' "

Matthew gave him a little poke.

"James printed the letters. He didn't know Benjamin had written them," said Mrs. Miller.

"Really?" Beast said again, looking up at the picture.

"His brother was angry when he found out," Mrs. Miller said. "He even gave Benjamin a smack."

Beast smiled, thinking about it.

Dawn held up her hand. "Hey. I just thought of something new. Something about Beast."

Beast closed his eyes. Don't tell, he wanted to say.

"Beast is just like Benjamin," Dawn said.

Beast opened his eyes again.

"Hey," said Timothy Barbiero. He pointed to Beast's sneakers. "Orange dots."

Mrs. Miller was looking at him.

When she saw him looking back, she smiled. "He does have good ideas," she said. "I bet he'll be an inventor just like Ben."

They went back up the stairs again.

Dawn marched along next to him. "Maybe you're like Benjamin Franklin," she said. "But don't think you get the prize."

"I need it," Beast began. "I really need it."

"That baby is mine," Dawn said.

Chapter 9

They were at the zoo.

Beast was watching a polar bear. The bear had lots of white fur.

He was ready to dive off a cliff into the water.

Polar bears were great swimmers. Holly had told him that.

He could see Holly across the way.

She waved when she saw him.

He waved back.

She was edging around toward him.

She was probably going to tell him about the rest of the zoo.

She came toward him. Orange was all over her mouth. A Blast-Off Bar, he thought.

"The Philadelphia Zoo was made in the 1800s," she told him. "It's really famous. The animals feel at home here."

"I thought you'd tell me something like that," he said.

"There are sixteen hundred animals, you know." Holly was nodding. "You'll even be able to see a sloth. I read all about it."

"Nice," he said. "I never saw one before."

"You know what?" she asked.

He swallowed. Maybe she had seen the bike after all.

"About Benjamin Franklin . . . ," Holly began.

He took a breath.

"You remind me of him," Holly said.

"Really?" He watched the bear swimming around in the water. The bear's fur was all slicked back now.

"That's what Dawn said," he told her. He felt great.

They walked a couple of steps. They could see a bear asleep on a ledge.

"Do you remember when you made a snake path in the yard?" Holly asked.

"Too bad there weren't any snakes." He leaned forward. "I'm going to be an inventor when I grow up."

Holly looked serious. "That's good. Sometimes I worry about you."

"Don't worry," he said. "I'll probably be famous."

Holly laughed. "Maybe."

She leaned forward too. She had a bunch of freckles on her nose.

He had never really seen them before.

"You know what?" he said. "Maybe you'll be a teacher."

Holly opened her mouth. "That's the best thing to be. Just like Ms. Rooney. I never thought of that before."

"Right," Beast said. He wanted to say, like Mrs. Miller too.

But Holly wouldn't know that Mrs. Miller wasn't so bad after all.

"Thanks, Beast," she said.

He nodded. They were walking away from the bears now.

"We'll look for a sloth next." She was smiling. "A teacher. That's a new thing for me."

"I painted your bike," he said.

Holly stepped back. "Are you crazy?"

"It's really a mess now," Beast said. "An orange mess."

Matthew came up in back of them. "You told her?"

Holly's hands were on her hips.

"It's not bad," Matthew said. "I like it."

"Well . . . ," Holly began.

"Don't worry," Beast said. "I'm going to get you a bike."

"How?" Holly asked.

"I'm going to win—" He stopped. He shook his head. "I'm not going to win one."

"No," Matthew said.

"My bike looks like your orange dot sneakers?" Holly asked.

"Yes," said Matthew.

"I guess so," Beast said.

"Orange like an orange Blast-Off Bar?"

Beast nodded.

Holly tapped him on the shoulder with

her book. "I was right," she said. "You're just like Benjamin Franklin."

Beast swallowed.

"Don't worry," she said. "Orange is my favorite color."

Chapter 10

They were sitting at a long picnic table.

Beast took a look at the Delaware River. Ships were tied up at the dock.

Out on the water, a bunch of guys were rowing. They were in a long, skinny boat.

"You know, those boats are called sculls," Holly said.

Beast rapped on Matthew's head with his knuckles. "Is there a skull in there?" he asked.

Then he opened his lunch bag. He had an egg salad sandwich with apple slices on top.

"Want some?" he asked Matthew. "It's my new invention. Not so hot, though."

"I'll try it," Dawn said.

"Good," he told her. "It's an apple-egg sandwich. New name."

Dawn handed him a cream cheese and strawberry jelly sandwich.

It used to be his favorite. But now he was going to try something different every day.

Matthew had tuna fish, of course.

Mrs. Miller had peanut butter.

Benjamin Lee was sitting across from him. He was eating a potato salad sandwich.

Benjamin was going to be an inventor too.

Beast sat back. The rowers were going so fast they were almost out of sight.

He wondered who was going to win the bike.

He opened his mouth. "Listen," he told Mrs. Miller. "Our report was all mixed up."

"I know." Mrs. Miller grinned. "I can hear reports," she said. "Even when I'm sleeping."

Beast ducked his head.

"Still, you tried."

"That's true," Matthew said. "That's really true."

Mrs. Miller took another bite of her peanut butter sandwich. "Don't worry," she said.

Beast waved his hand. "My bike isn't so bad."

Matthew signed. "Mine neither."

Holly leaned across the table. "Mine is probably great."

"I was thinking about something," said Mrs. Miller. "I was thinking that everybody likes a prize."

"Yes," said Dawn Bosco. "I could use another bike."

"I bought prizes for everyone," Mrs. Miller said.

"You must be rich," said Matthew. "Bikes cost a lot of money."

Mrs. Miller looked surprised. "Not bikes."

Beast opened his mouth again. "Not bikes?"

He watched another bunch of rowers go past.

No bike prize, he thought. There never was a bike.

"How did we get the idea there was a bike?" he asked Matthew.

"Because you weren't listening," Dawn said. She was trying to look as if she knew everything. Too bad she had apple-egg on her face.

"You know," Holly was saying, "all the men who were making the new laws for the—"

"Constitution," Timothy broke in.

Holly nodded. "Yes. They really listened to each other. That's how they came up with such great stuff."

Dawn was still frowning. "What about my bike? I was counting on a new one."

"Sorry," Beast said. Then he had an idea. "I could paint your bike."

Dawn thought for a moment. "Not bad." She nodded at him. "How about purple?"

"Great color," said Beast.

"Two more minutes," Ms. Rooney called from the other end of the table. "We're on our way to see the United States Mint. It's where they make our money."

"A book," said Mrs. Miller. "The prize is a book."

"Books?" said Beast.

Mrs. Miller smiled. "I knew you'd love that." She pushed her glasses up. "It's *Olden Days in Old Philadelphia*."

Beast bit his lip. He didn't want to look at Matthew.

He knew Matthew would be laughing.

"I'm astounded," he said after a minute.

Maybe he would even read it.

He stood up.

He tossed his lunch bag in the basket.

They headed for the bus.

"Wait up," said Mrs. Miller. "I'm coming too."

Beast took another step.

Next to him Matthew sighed.

But they waited for Mrs. Miller to catch up.

"Remember her car?" Beast said. "Plain old black."

Matthew nodded.

"Maybe she'd like some polka dots."

He was going to ask her. After all, it was Something New Week at the Polk Street School.

The Polk Street
Guide to
Philadelphia

The Polk Street Kids' Favorite Places to See in Philadelphia (listed in alphabetical order)

Ms. Rooney says:

"Get on your traveling shoes. Tell us what you like about Philadelphia, the City of Brotherly Love. . . ."

"My turn first," says Dawn Bosco.

You could start at *Independence National Historical Park*. Ms. Rooney says it's the birthplace of our country. It's a square mile.

Wear your walking shoes. Stop at the Visitor Center for a map. See a film called *Independence*. Buy a tiny Liberty Bell at the bookstore. You'll find other maps and books too.

Visitor Center, Third and Chestnut Streets, (215) 597-8974

Web site: www.libertynet.org/~inhp

Emily Arrow says:

See the *Liberty Bell Pavilion*. The Liberty Bell is there in a special glass case. It was made in 1752. Ms. Rooney said the bell is a symbol. It tells us all Americans are free. The bell used to be rung for special happenings, like the reading of the Declaration of

Independence. The sad part is that the bell cracked in 1846. It can't be rung anymore.

Market Street between Fifth and Sixth Streets, (215) 597-8974

Report by Richard Best and Matthew J. Jackson:

See *Independence Hall*. It's filled with history! A group of men met here in 1776. They signed the Declaration of Independence. It said that Americans were free from England.

Eleven years later they met to say we were a country now, the United States. They wrote a paper called the Constitution. It gave us laws.

Guess who was there! George Washington and Benjamin Franklin. You can see inkstands and sandboxes that they used to blot their papers. You'll see long green tablecloths too. They dragged on the floor so the men could wrap up their legs and stay warm.

Outside, next to the statue of Washington, is a spot where some of our presidents have stood: Lincoln, Kennedy, and Clinton. Dawn Bosco says she stood there too.

Chestnut Street between Fifth and Sixth Streets, (215) 597-8974

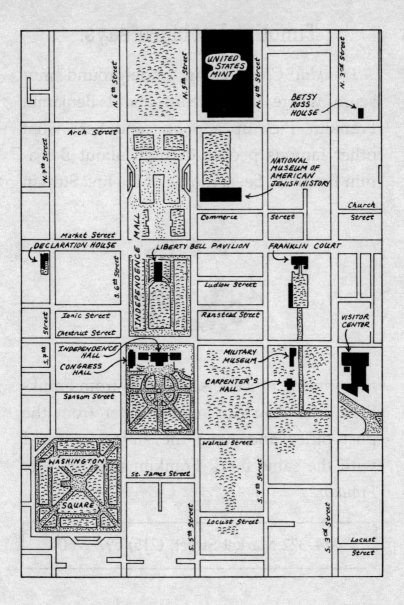

Timothy Barbiero says:

Franklin Court is an underground museum where you'll learn about Benjamin Franklin. Pick up a phone and hear what other famous people thought about Benjamin Franklin. See a movie of his life. Stop in

the printing office to see a press from Franklin's time. You can mail a letter from the post office and have the stamp canceled with the same mark Franklin used: *B. Free Franklin.*

314–322 Market Street, (215) 597-2760

Noah Green likes:

The old tools in *Carpenter's Hall*. The hall was built in 1770. The First Continental Congress met here to talk about the problems with England.

320 Chestnut Street, (215) 597-8974

Beast says:

If you like uniforms and weapons, see the *New Hall Military Museum*. There's even a flintlock musket from 1763. *Paboom!*

Chestnut Street, east of Fourth Street, (215) 597-8974

Jill Simon wants you to:

Take a quick walk through *Congress Hall*. George Washington became president for the second time right in the Senate chamber upstairs.

Chestnut Street and Sixth Street,
(215) 597-8974

Linda Lorca writes:

Thomas Jefferson lived at *Declaration House* in June of 1776. He worked here on the Declaration of Independence. You can see a copy of it . . . with the cross-outs! You can also see how the rooms looked.

Seventh and Market Streets, (215) 597-8974

Beast asks:

How about *Fireman's Hall Museum*? See a firehouse that was built in 1901. It has old fire trucks and uniforms.

147 North Second Street, (215) 923-1438

Emily Arrow likes:

The *Betsy Ross House.* I read a book about her life once. People are not really sure if she lived here. They're not even sure if she

really made the first flag. Visit the house anyway. You'll see how things looked in the days of Betsy Ross. You can also visit her grave next door. She's buried with her third husband.

239 Arch Street, (215) 627-5343

Alex Walker writes:

I liked the *Afro-American Historical and Cultural Museum*. You'll see arts and crafts and learn about African American history.

Don't miss the gift shop. It has carvings and beautiful jewelry from Africa.

Seventh and Arch Streets, (215) 574-0380

Ms. Rooney says:

You won't want to miss the *Philadelphia Zoo*. Watch the gorillas and other primates in their jungle, and the rhinos, giraffes, and zebras on the African plain. Polar bears dive off cliffs. Catch the sea lion show.

Girard Avenue and Thirty-fourth Street, (215) 243-1100

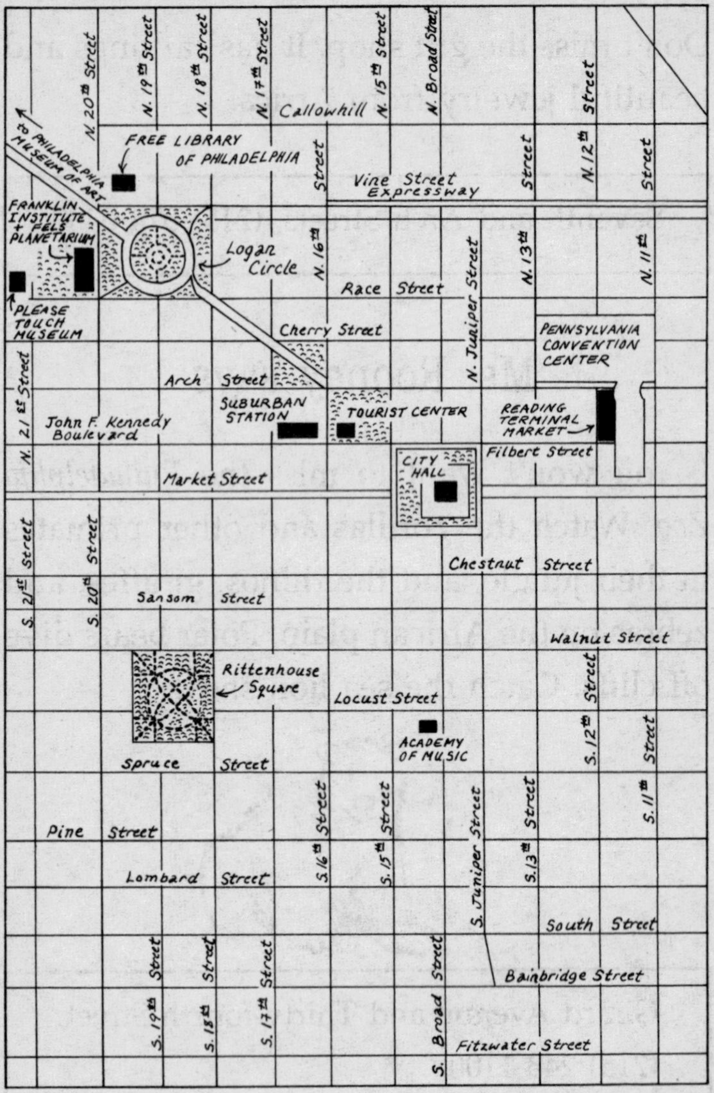

N. 20th Street
N. 19th Street
N. 18th Street
N. 17th Street
N. 15th Street
N. Broad Street
N. 12th Street
Callowhill
to Philadelphia Museum of Art
Free Library of Philadelphia
N. 16th Street
Vine Street Expressway
N. 13th Street
Street
Franklin Institute + Fels Planetarium
Logan Circle
N. Juniper Street
N. 11th Street
Please Touch Museum
Race Street
Cherry Street
Pennsylvania Convention Center
N. 21st Street
Arch Street
Suburban Station
Tourist Center
Reading Terminal Market
John F. Kennedy Boulevard
City Hall
Filbert Street
Market Street
S. 21st Street
S. 20th Street
Chestnut Street
Sansom Street
Walnut Street
Rittenhouse Square
Locust Street
S. 12th Street
Academy of Music
Spruce Street
S. 11th Street
S. 16th Street
S. 15th Street
S. Juniper Street
S. 13th Street
Pine Street
Lombard Street
South Street
S. 19th Street
S. 18th Street
S. 17th Street
S. Broad Street
Bainbridge Street
Fitzwater Street

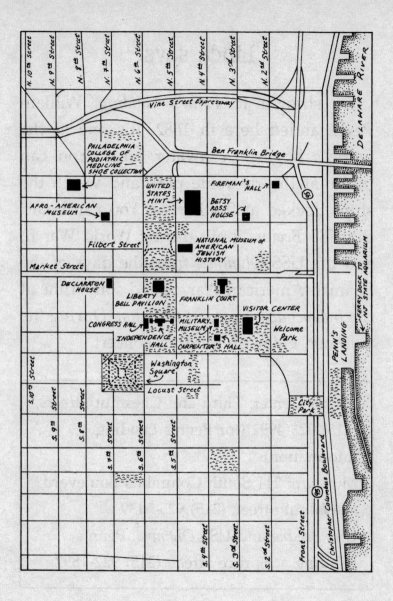

Linda says:

Go straight to *Penn's Landing*. William Penn landed here in 1682. It's one of the world's largest freshwater ports. You can picnic at the riverside park and watch the ships docked at the harbor. You can board the USS *Becuna*, built during World War II, and the USS *Olympia*, from the days of the Spanish-American War. Spend some time at the *Independence Seaport Museum*. During the summer, enjoy an outdoor concert.

Visitor Center: Third and Chestnut Streets, (215) 923-4992 (for Penn's Landing information)
Museum: 211 South Columbus Boulevard at Walnut Street, (215) 925-5439
USS *Becuna* and USS *Olympia*: Penn's Landing at Spruce Street, (215) 922-1892

Dawn's grandmother Noni says:

Not far from the landing is *Welcome Park*. William Penn once lived here. *(Welcome* was the name of the ship that brought him to America.) On the pavement is a huge map. It's Philadelphia the way it looked when Penn was alive. You'll also read about the events of Penn's life on a time line.

Sansom Street at Second Street

Jill writes:

From Penn's Landing catch the Riverlink ferry to the *New Jersey State Aquarium*. You'll cross the Delaware River in ten minutes. Don't miss the interactive show at the aquarium. You might be able to pet a shark. You'll see some other fish too . . . six thousand of them. A diver will answer your questions using a scubaphone.

Riverlink: Penn's Landing at Walnut Street, (215) 925-LINK
Aquarium: 1 Riverside Drive, Camden, NJ, (609) 365-3300

Miss Kara, the art teacher, doesn't want you to miss:

Seeing a play at the *Annenberg Center Theater for Children*. Especially wonderful is the five-day Philadelphia International Theater Festival for Children. It is held over the last weekend in May and features music, dance, puppets, and the circus.

Thirty-seventh and Walnut Streets,
(215) 898-6791

Miss Bailey, the librarian, writes:

The *Free Library Children's Department* has more than a hundred thousand books for children. There are films to see, stories to hear, and a collection of old books that your parents will love too.

Nineteenth Street and Benjamin Franklin Parkway, (215) 686-5369

Timothy writes:

My favorite is the *Academy of Natural Sciences*. It's a dinosaur place with fossils and skeletons and dinosaur teeth! It also has stuffed animals in their natural settings from all over the world.

Nineteenth Street and Benjamin Franklin Parkway, (215) 299-1020

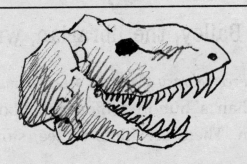

Sherri Dent says:

I guess you'll be surprised to hear that I wasn't afraid at the *Insectarium*. We saw a collection of about fifteen hundred insects, from teeny-tiny ones to giant centipedes. It has a great souvenir shop too!

8046 Frankfurt Avenue, Northeast
Philadelphia, (215) 338-3000

Emily says:

My little sister Stacy would love the *Please Touch Museum*. It's meant for children seven

and younger. It's an interactive museum:
You can walk through the world of *Where
the Wild Things Are*, by Maurice Sendak,
shop or work in a miniature supermarket,
and do other things. See a performance in
the theater—magic, puppets, sing-alongs.

210 North Twenty-first Street,
(215) 963-0667

Timothy writes:

Do you like money as much as I do? See
the *United States Mint*. It's the largest
money-making place in the world. Buy special shiny coins in the gift shop.

Arch and Fifth Streets, (215) 597-7350

Alex says:

If you like statues, see the thirty-seven-foot statue of William Penn on top of the largest *City Hall* in the country (642 rooms). Take an elevator to the observation deck at the foot of the statue. You'll see the city from

up on top. Nearby is a huge piece of art that's really different. It's the forty-five-foot *Clothespin*, designed by Claes Oldenburg.

City Hall: Broad and Market Streets, (215) 686-2840

Clothespin: Fifteenth and Market Streets

Linda likes:

The *Reading Terminal Market*. It's a great place for food. There's everything from hot pretzels to Amish shoofly pie. You can

taste Greek, Italian, Mexican, and Indian food, and many others. Wander around the tiny stalls to look for something special.

Twelfth and Filbert Streets, (215) 922-2317

Linda also says:

Jewish people have lived in America since 1654. You can learn about their lives at the *National Museum of American Jewish History*. See films and paintings. Imagine how it felt to live three hundred years ago or during the Revolutionary War.

---

55 North Fifth Street, (215) 923-3811

Derrick Grace writes:

Climb into a steam locomotive or sit in the cockpit of a jet plane at the *Franklin Institute Science Museum*, which is named after Ben and shows some of his inventions. There are also computers to test, a weather station to see, and a huge pinball machine to

play. You can visit the *Fels Planetarium* to learn about space and the stars.

Twentieth Street and Benjamin Franklin Parkway, (215) 448-1200

Dawn says:

Check out the *Shoe Museum* at the Pennsylvania College of Podiatric Medicine. There must be five hundred pairs of shoes from all over the world. Some of them are five thousand years old. Some of them are modern and belonged to famous sports stars.

Eighth and Race Streets, (215) 625-5243

Matthew says:

You won't mind hanging out at the *Smith Playground* in Fairmount Park. Bring a picnic lunch to spread out on a table. Try the jun-

gle gym, or take a swim. Inside the Smith Mansion are some great playrooms for little kids.

> Near Fairmount Park, Thirty-third and Oxford Streets, (215) 765-4325

Mrs. Clark loves:

The *Philadelphia Museum of Art.* It's huge, and has statues and works of art. There are rooms that were moved from a temple in India, a cloister in France, and a four-hundred-year-old Chinese palace. Part of the fun is racing up the ninety-nine steps to the front door. Sylvester Stallone was filmed doing that in the movie *Rocky.*

> Twenty-sixth Street and Benjamin Franklin Parkway, (215) 763-8100

Jill loves:

Food! And in Philadelphia, the official sandwich is a hoagie. . . . Try one at *Lee's Hoagie House*. It will be filled with pepper ham, salami, tomato, lettuce, hot peppers . . . and don't forget the onions. Another Philadelphia special is a cheesesteak. Try one on a roll at *Pat's King of Steaks*. You'll love the melted cheese and fried onions.

Then drive to the town of *Lititz*, which is about two hours away. The first thing you'll notice is the wonderful smell of chocolate. It's coming from the *Wilbur Chocolate Company's Candy Americana Museum and Candy*

Store. Stop there and see how candy is made. Get a free sample too. Then head for the *Julius Sturgis Pretzel House.* Philadelphians love those fat pretzels. Watch them being twisted and baked. You can even try to twist one yourself.

Lee's Hoagie House, 44 South Seventeenth Street, (215) 564-1264
Pat's King of Steaks, 1237 East Passyunk Avenue, (215) 339-9872
Wilbur Chocolate Company's Candy Americana Museum and Candy Store, 48 North Broad Street, Lititz, (717) 626-1131
Julius Sturgis Pretzel House, 219 East Main Street, Lititz, (717) 626-4354

About the Author/About the Artist

Patricia Reilly Giff is the author of more than fifty books for young readers, including *Lily's Crossing*, a *Boston Globe–Horn Book* Fiction Honor Book; the Kids of the Polk Street School books; the Lincoln Lions Marching Band books; and the Polka Dot Private Eye books. She lives in Weston, Connecticut.

Blanche Sims has illustrated all the Polk Street books. She lives in Westport, Connecticut.